Magical Mix-Ups

D0779386

Friends and Fashion

First U.S. edition 2012

ISBN 978-0-7636-6166-3

12 13 14 15 16 17 BVG 10 9 8 7 6 5 4 3 2 1

Printed in Berryville, VA, U.S.A.

This book was typeset in Bell MT.
The illustrations were created digitally.

Nosy Crow
an imprint of
Candlewick Press
99 Dover Street
Somerville, Massachusetts 02144

www.nosycrow.com
www.candlewick.com

Magical Mix-Ups

Friends and Fashion

Marnie Edwards * Leigh Hodgkinson

nosy crow

An imprint of Candlewick Press

Who's Who in MIXTOPIA

Emerald the Witch

Princess Sapphire

Boris—Emerald's toad

Who's who at the GRAND PALACE

Empress Maisie

Poppy

Lulu

You'll need these. . . .

Drawing

TOOLS

Using different tools helps
create great drawings.

PENCIL

COLORED PENCIL

CRAYON

Decorating TOOLS

Use these to add extra SPARKLE and MAGIC.

Sequins

Pencil rubbings

Tinfoil

Glitter

Drawing Tips
Turn to the back of the book for drawing and design ideas!

Glitter
at the
READY

GET
SET

GO!

Chapter 1

The BEST of Friends

Add doors
and windows
to the castle.

Who is playing by the fountains?

Where does
this path go?

Add patterned hills in the background.

Draw wonky stepping-stones up to Emerald's house.

Princess Sapphire and Emerald the Witch are best friends. They live next door to each other in Mixtopia, a land where anything can happen, and usually does.

Sapphire loves clothes, shoes, and looking neat.

Clothes

Shoes

Draw Sapphire's perfect hair.

Emerald loves her pet toad, Boris, and can't remember if she owns a hairbrush.

Draw Emerald's messy hair.

What do you think?

HAIRBRUSH?

YES ☐

NO ☐

Color in Emerald's witchy outfit.

They may be very different, but both girls love magazines and comics!

Draw Boris up to no good!

Who is on the front cover?

CROWNS & SPARKLE

how to make your crown shimmer & SPARKLE

TOADSTOOLS & TIARAS

FREE GIFT

What is the free gift?

Add more magazines to the pile.

What is this comic called?

Sapphire's favorite magazine is *Kind Hearts and Coronets*. "Ooh, a quiz!" she cries.

Fill in the princess quiz.

Which Princess are you?

Do you like:

A) sparkly glittery things?

B) petting slugs?

Do you live in:

A) a castle?

B) a spaceship?

Do you wear:

A a tiara?

B flippers?

☐
☐

Do you:

A giggle and squeal a lot?

B burp and sniffle a lot?

☐
☐

Number of A's

Number of B's

If you had mostly A's, you are a very good princess.

If you had mostly B's, you are a terrible princess.

Draw a very good princess here.

Draw a terrible princess here.

Then Boris sneezes loudly. "Bless you," says Emerald.

Boris is just blowing
his nose when Sapphire
suddenly squeaks
with excitement.
"Look at this, Em!"
she cries, waving
her magazine
around madly.

Color in Sapphire's hair and crown.

Draw
Sapphire's
excited face.

ATTENTION

all you crafty princesses!

Empress **maisie**

needs an outfit for her

6th birthday party.

and she needs **YOU** to make it for her.

The winning outfit will be chosen at a

FANTABULOUS

Fashion show at the

GRAND **Palace**

in **2** days' time!

Ready, steady—Sew!

Design the magazine border!

Princess Sapphire's eyes are shining.
"I can't wait to get started!" she says.
Suddenly, Boris the Toad sneezes so hard
he falls off Emerald's shoulder!
Boris doesn't look so good.

Color in Sapphire.

Finish the tumble line.

Draw a box of tissues for Boris.

Chapter 2

BuTToNS
and
BoBBiNS

Poor Boris has gone to bed. "Time for a get-well potion," says Emerald. "I'll need some things. . . ." She makes a shopping list and sets off for the city.

What is on TV?

Add more zaps.

ICE CREAM

What flavor is the ice cream? Color it in.

Draw her shopping basket.

Draw Emerald's broomstick by the door.

Put on Emerald's cloak.

Meanwhile, Sapphire is rummaging through the Royal Scrap Box. There are lots of lovely things she can use for Empress Maisie's outfit in there. . . .

Off flies Emerald!

Design pretty patterns on the fabric scraps.

Add more piles of buttons.

Add your own button rubbings.

What is Sapphire holding?

Decorate the side of the button box.

Sapphire then heads off to find the Royal Button Box. What a treasure trove!

"Now, what would little Maisie like to wear?" she wonders.

She looks at the magazine again and spots some tiny writing she missed before.

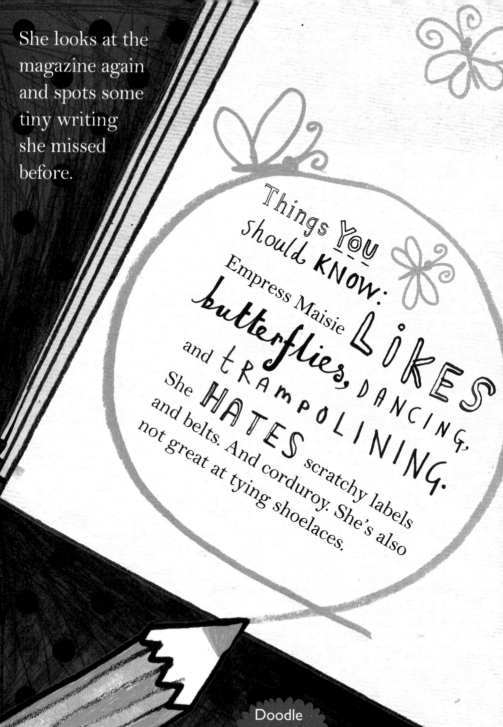

Things **You** should **KNOW:**
Empress Maisie **LiKES** **butterflies,** DANCING, and tRAMPOLINING. She **HATES** scratchy labels and belts. And corduroy. She's also not great at tying shoelaces.

Doodle more butterflies.

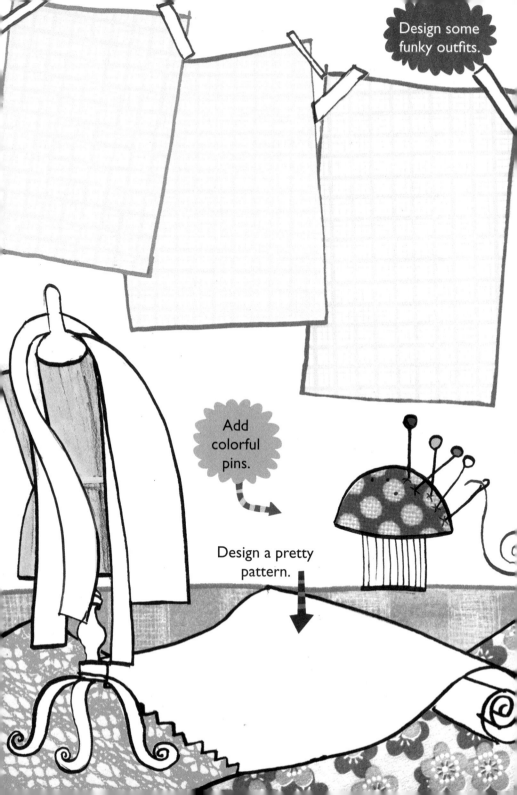

Design some funky outfits.

Add colorful pins.

Design a pretty pattern.

"Aha!" cries Princess Sapphire, settling herself at her worktable. "I've got the perfect idea!"

Give Sapphire an idea lightbulb.

More stitching, please

As Sapphire gets to work, Boris sighs in his sleep and turns over. . . .

Chapter 3

A

FLYING

visit

Emerald looks at the ingredients she needs for
Boris's get-well potion. They're mostly disgusting.
"Rather you than me, Boris," she says.

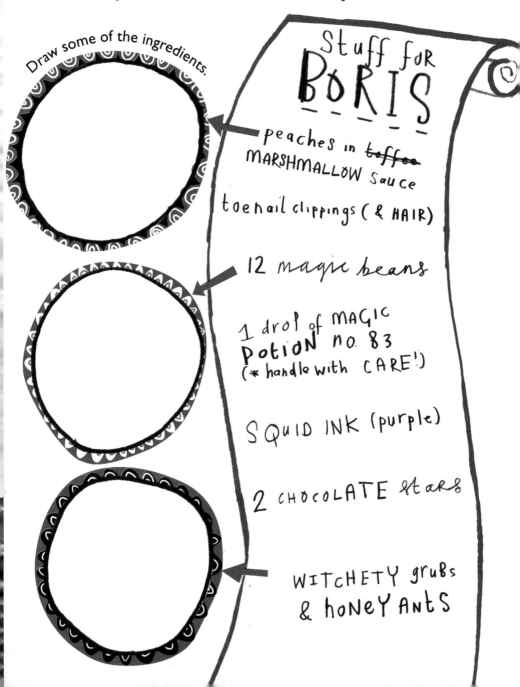

Draw some of the ingredients.

Stuff for
BORIS

peaches in ~~toffee~~
MARSHMALLOW sauce

toenail clippings (& HAIR)

12 magic beans

1 drop of MAGIC
POTION no. 83
(* handle with CARE!)

SQUID INK (purple)

2 CHOCOLATE stars

WITCHETY gruBs
& hoNeY ANtS

Draw your made-up stuff.

What else would a witch have on her shopping list?

GENERAL Stuff

First, Emerald heads for the deli counter.
Her mouth waters — what amazing delicacies!

Add more jars and bottles to the shelves.

Fill the trays with goodies.

CHOCOLATE stars

deep-fried snails

magic beans

THE MAGIC deli

She might just treat herself to a deep-fried snail or two, even if they will spoil her lunch.

Emerald feels excited as she pushes open the door to the Beauty Room. Everything sparkles and shines, and the witch behind the counter has AMAZING hair!

Add more bows.

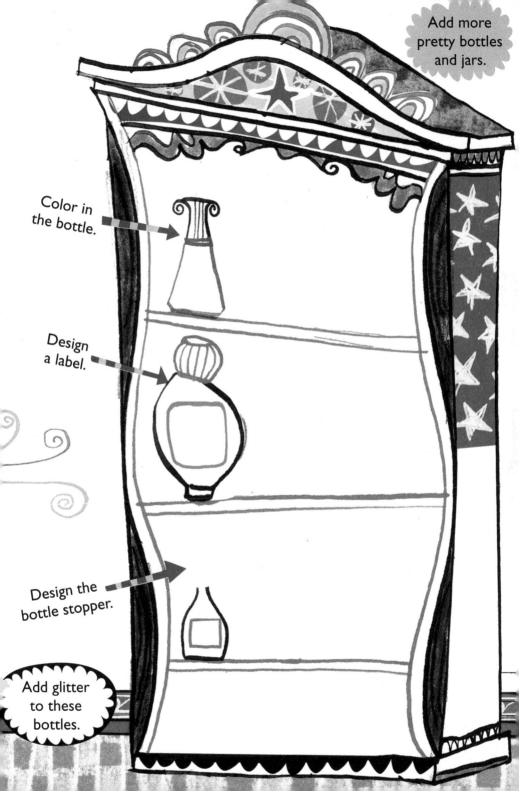

Add more pretty bottles and jars.

Color in the bottle.

Design a label.

Design the bottle stopper.

Add glitter to these bottles.

What is reflected in the mirrors?

Draw a fancy frame.

"My, these snails are chewy," says Emerald as she goes into the Beauty Room.

Once Emerald has everything she needs, she heads home to her laboratory. "Bubble, bubble, boil and er . . ." she says. "Oh, I can never remember how that goes!"

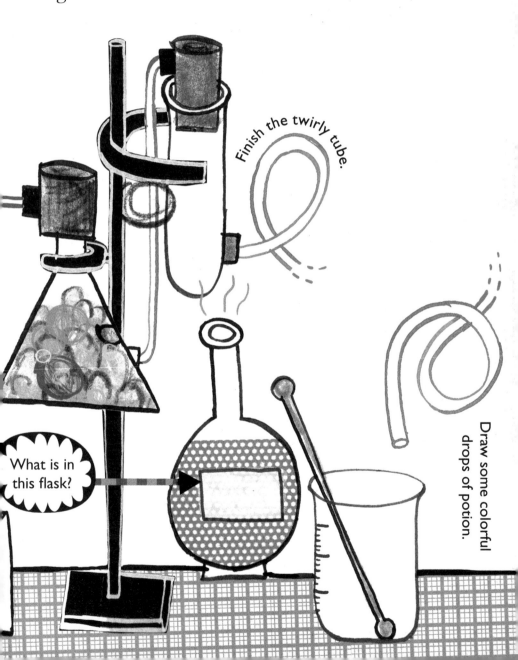

Finish the twirly tube.

What is in this flask?

Draw some colorful drops of potion.

One small explosion later, the get-well potion is
ready! Emerald carefully takes it to Boris, who doesn't
look very pleased to see her, or the big spoon. . . .

Chapter 4

UP, UP, and AWAY

Are there stars in the sky?

Has Sapphire got a bedtime drink?

Design a funky comforter for Sapphire.

Night is falling, and at the castle, Princess Sapphire is getting ready for bed. She has pricked her fingers with her needle so many times, they're like pincushions. "Move over, Sleeping Beauty," she says, climbing into bed.

Write a
big yawn in
here.

Design some
princess
pajamas.

Sapphire is woken up bright and early by
Emerald landing on her carpet. "I do wish you'd
use the door occasionally," Sapphire grumbles.

But her friend isn't listening. "Boris is better!" Emerald cries happily. But just then, Boris gives an ENORMOUS sneeze. "Well, almost better," she adds.

"We've come to help you," says Emerald. "We've got some great ideas for Maisie's outfit. . . ."

What Outfit WOULD YOU make?

"But I've already finished!" says Sapphire, pointing to her dressmaker's dummy. "Look!"

Who is sitting on the pincushion?

It's time to leave for the Grand Palace. The Royal Hot-Air Balloon is ready and waiting on the lawn, and Boris is wearing his best scarf.

Add more cute creatures.

Add trees and flowers on the hills.

Who is flying in the sky?

Oops! What has Boris dropped?

Is this a rain cloud?

Draw more treetops.

Soon they are high in the sky.
"Watch out for those flying ponies!" says Sapphire.

Draw
more flying
ponies.

Look!
A rainbow!

Just then, they spy Empress Maisie's Grand Palace down below. It's almost time for the Fashion Show!

Use pencil rubbings to decorate the Grand Palace.

Color in the flag and draw some trees.

Chapter 5

MODEL
Behavior

The balloon lands gently on the palace lawn.

Why is Empress Maisie looking grumpy?

Reason 1

Reason 2

Reason 3

Empress Maisie is waiting to greet them. She looks a little grumpy, though!

The Fashion Show will take place in a huge tent.
Inside, everyone is rushing around, getting things ready.

Add more Royal banners.

Draw more grand flower displays in the vases.

Princess Sapphire peeks into the dressing room and gasps. Ooh-la-la, the glamour!

Draw the models' reflections in the mirrors.

Draw the missing shoes to make pairs.

What else is on the dressing table?

A girl with very long hair comes over.
"Hello," she says. "I'm Poppy.
That's my outfit over there."

POPPY's outfit

entry Number **1**

Where is Boris hiding?

Finish coloring in Poppy's outfit.

Add more colorful ribbons.

What shoes would you put with Poppy's outfit?

Add stars to the jacket.

LuLu's outfit
eNTRY NuMBER 2

What color would you make Lulu's hat?

Add more polka dots.

What outfit would Boris like to wear?

Is Boris holding something?

"And that's mine next to it,"
says another girl, pointing.
"My name's Lulu. I love your toad!"
Boris beams with pleasure before
giving a HUGE sneeze.

Decorate
Sapphire's
skirt.

Sapphire introduces herself nervously . . .

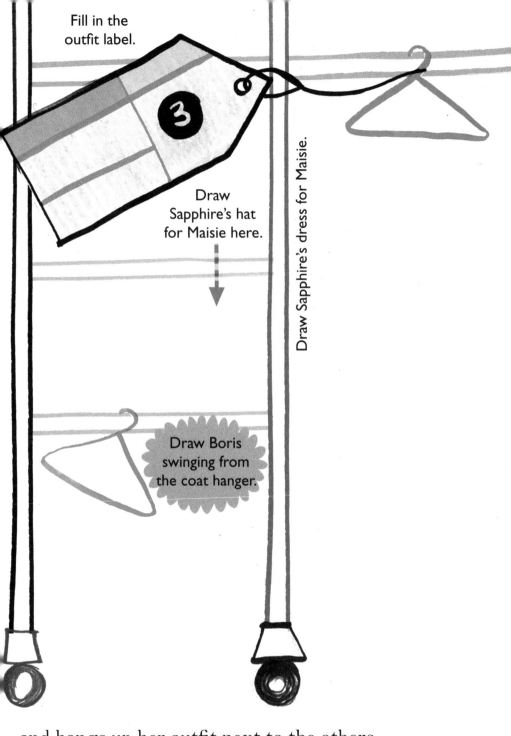

Fill in the outfit label.

3

Draw Sapphire's hat for Maisie here.

Draw Sapphire's dress for Maisie.

Draw Boris swinging from the coat hanger.

and hangs up her outfit next to the others.

Now nothing could
possibly go wrong.

Could it?

In each section,
draw possible
things that could
go wrong.

Chapter 6

A Fashion FIASCO

Draw more fashionable ladies watching the show.

Is she wearing dangly earrings?

Give the ladies big sunglasses.

Emerald decides to take her hat to the dressing room. As she opens the door, Boris sneezes so hard that he flies off Emerald's shoulder again and knocks all the outfits into a pile on the floor.

Emerald tries to put them back together again,
but she is not sure she has gotten it right. . . .

"Er, Sapphy . . ." Back at her seat, Emerald tries to tell her friend about the mix-up, but just then, the lights go down, the music starts, and the Fashion Show gets under way. . . .

Draw in the models' hair.

Sapphire, Poppy, and Lulu stare at the models in horror. All the outfits are muddled up!

But then the crowd starts clapping and stamping their feet in delight. The outfits are a huge hit!

"They're fabulous—all of them,"
exclaims Empress Maisie.
"Now I have three birthday
outfits instead of one!"

She is so happy that she
throws a special trampolining
party to celebrate!

Add more
yummy things
to the picnic.

Draw
everyone's
shoes lined
up here.

Draw bouncy boing lines.

Who else is bouncing on the trampoline?

"I'm sorry I mixed everything up," says Emerald to Sapphire as they head home in the Royal Hot-Air Balloon.

Look! Poppy is riding home on a magic bicycle.

Lulu is riding a flying pony.

Can you add tiny tinfoil stars?

Draw the turrets of the Grand Palace down below.

"That's all right," says Sapphire, and she gives her best friend a big hug. "But remind me never to ask you for any fashion tips!"

The Big Picture
Draw your favorite moments from the book, and glue on any fun decorative bits.

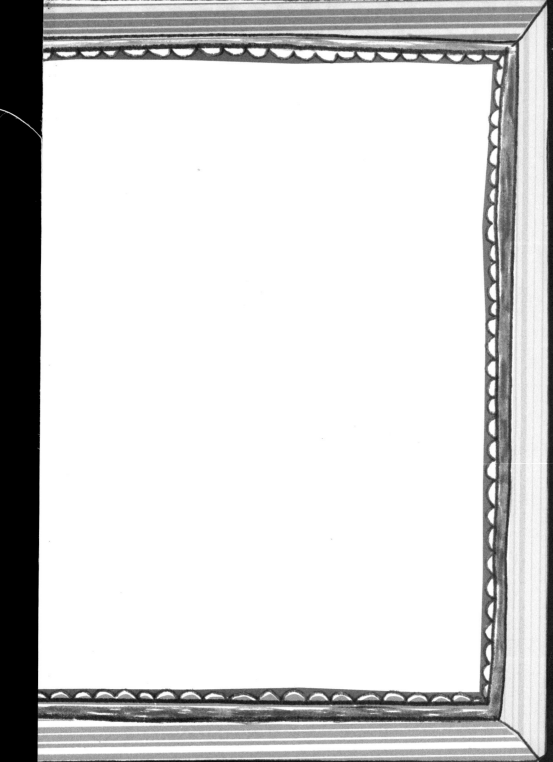

picture GLOSSARY

If you need a helping hand thinking of things to draw, then check these ideas out!

royal fish

sneeze effect

ATcHOOO!

What's on TV?

WITCH FACTOR

stars

creatures

magic beans

flying witch

Boris's dream

KING BORIS

magic bicycle

Sapphire's bedtime drink

trees

flowers